Secret Ingredient

Femdom Hypnosis and Mind Control Micro-Fiction

S.B.

Disclaimer

This is a work of fiction. Names, characters, business, events, and incidents are the products of the author's imagination. Any resemblance to actual persons, living or dead, or actual events is purely coincidental. All characters are over 18.

Feed your mind with her suggestions.

Thank you to all patrons of Spell... B-O-U-N-D.

Table of Contents

Introduction

Imagination is the nourishment of the mind. Without it, we're nothing but thinking machines, trapped in endless routines. The best way to break free is to open your mind to the powerful suggestions of hypnotic women who always know what is best for you. Let them feed your innermost desires.

The stories in this volume were written between April 3rd, and May 27th, 2022, and published on my personal website – Spell... B-O-U-N-D – as part of my daily 55 Words Challenge that's been running for almost seven years now. Have fun.

One Word of This Story…

One word of this story will trigger you.

A single word will turn you into my slave.

I won't tell you what it is, but your subconscious will recognize it and react accordingly.

It already happened, didn't it? You are mine to command.

Only another word can release you now, but it's not here. Kneel.

Nothing to Hide

Victor blushed as his naked body was thoroughly examined.

"You were right," Justine said. "You really have nothing to hide."

"Thank you, but can I get dressed now? It's cold," he replied.

"Not until I test a few more triggers, pet," Kayla smirked, pocket watch in hand.

Justine loved it. Victor's ass not so much.

Ridiculous Comment

David had read many dubious comments on his profile over the years, but this one was laughable. The three words were:

Strip. Camera. Outside.

"Yeah, right", he muttered, not realizing he was already on the porch. The moonlight reflected on his naked ass as he stared into his phone.

"Another successful suggestion," Mistress Melinda smirked.

With a Straight Face

Everyone can say "I love you" with a straight face. Everyone can say "I hate you" with a straight face.

Only deeply entranced people can say "I am your mindfucked pussy bitch that howls at the moon on command while my ass is being fucked by an imaginary dildo" without laughing.

I just tried. Fuck!

Nine Months

"Congratulations, it's a girl!" Judith said.

"Can I hold her?" Dennis asked.

"Of course."

"Thank you. Hello, gorgeous. It's so nice to meet you. I can't believe you were inside me the last nine months."

"Neither can I," Judith giggled as he held the plastic doll. He really was the most suggestible toy of all.

Free Will

"You have no free will," Diana said, waving her pendant.

"That's not true," Jack said.

"It isn't?"

"No. I can choose not to be hypnotized. I can also refuse your suggestions if they're bad for me."

"Okay, so what are you going to do?"

"Become your mindless drone for the weekend."

"Good plan," she chuckled.

One of Those Days...

Harold's protests were relentless.

"Is everything okay with your husband?" Justine asked.

"Yeah. It's one of those days where he doesn't want to obey..." Karen replied.

"But why is he screaming at a wall?"

"I convinced him it's me."

"So dumb..."

"You too," Karen chuckled as her friend continued to talk to an empty sofa.

A Hypnotic Story

David read a hypnotic story and came.

Emily read a hypnotic story and came.

Terence read a hypnotic story and came.

Frank read a hypnotic story and came.

Albert read a hypnotic story and came.

Theresa read a hypnotic story and came.

I wrote the hypnotic story because my Mistress told me to. Still waiting...

The Last Time We Were Together

"Surprise!" Erin exclaimed.

"What are you doing here?" Nathan asked.

"Hey, is that any way to treat an old friend?"

"No offense but the last time we were together, you messed with my mind really good."

"Did I?"

"Yes. Don't you remember?"

"Vaguely, but here's the thing..."

"What?"

"This is the last time."

"Oh, fu..."

Lucky Her

The old mirror lay in pieces on the floor.

"Damn it!" Brandon said.

"Oh dear, bad luck for the rest of your life..." Martha said.

"Since when? The superstition is seven years."

"Since I said so and you believe everything I say..." she snapped her fingers.

"Yes, dear."

"Lucky me you're so suggestible," she thought.

Wrong Place

Marcus answered the door to find a beautiful redhead waiting.

"Yes?"

"I was told of a bedroom here..." she replied.

"House next door. You got the wrong place."

"I think I'm right. Do you live alone?"

"None of your business, sorry."

"It will be soon," she drew a pendant from her cleavage.

She was right.

Hypnotic Feedback

Vince stared angrily at the computer. The feedback he received was always the same: vague praise with no substance.

Except for that night.

The e-mail opened to a spiral, wrapped in another spiral that dulled his senses. The white words at the center read: good slave.

Yes, he was. Mindlessly, he started writing something new.

Light Show

Dan's kitchen lamp wouldn't stop flickering.

"You have to fix this!" Walter said.

"Agreed, but I need to check something first."

"What?"

"Anne said that if I looked at it long enough, I could go into trance."

"Really?"

"Yeah, so give me a couple of minutes."

"Okay."

They haven't left the house the whole weekend.

Come and See

"Honey, you're keeping the guests waiting" Lucy exclaimed.

"One second while I finish this..." Jeremy said.

"Writing erotic hypnosis stories again?"

"What? No! What gave you that idea?"

"Everybody knows your secret, hence the surprise."

"What surprise?"

"Come and see."

Pocket watches and spirals awaited him downstairs. It was going to be a beautiful weekend.

Gone for a While

"Welcome back," Gail said.

"What do you mean? I've been here the whole time!" Horace retorted.

"Actually, you've been gone for a while."

"Don't be ridiculous."

"What's the last thing you remember?"

"Driving here to give you your Christmas present, of course. Why?"

"Because it's already Easter, sweetie," she smirked, a metronome ticking behind her.

What Did You Do?

Dave and Walter blinked, awakening from their altered state of mind.

"Hey, boys," Anne said.

"You fixed the lamp," Dave noted.

"Yep."

"How long were we out?"

"Long enough for some hypnotic fun."

"What did you do?" Walter asked.

"What you should be asking is what you did to each other..."

The two men screamed.

Business as Usual

The tentacled thing looking at Dan was impossible to describe.

"What are you?" he asked.

"Nothing you can understand..." Caroline responded.

"Have I gone insane?"

"That's what people will think." She/it drew closer.

"What are you going to do now?"

"It's business as usual, dear. I'm hungry."

One by one his thoughts melted away.

The Experiment

Walter stared blankly at his computer screen. Nothing on the search results. The woman that had played with his mind for over a year was nowhere to be found.

"It's like she was never real," he muttered.

"That's because she wasn't," his twin sister smiled, standing behind him. The hypnotic experiment had been a success.

Drawn Her Way

Frank stared at Elsa's latest drawing and frowned.

"I'm sorry, but this is horrible."

"Why?"

"Because I don't look like this."

"You do when you're entranced."

"Entran...? Shit! Is that why I'm wearing a collar?"

"Yes, and if you keep complaining about my art..."

Elsa drew something new that afternoon. Frank looked good in diapers.

Not Fresh Enough

Valerie's cooking was getting worse each day.

"How is this possible?" Mick asked, spitting sausage on his plate.

"The ingredients weren't fresh" she replied.

"It tastes like old cock."

"How do you know that?"

"I don't remember."

"Good," she smiled, eyes on the bleeding wound on his crotch. The new drugs worked like a charm.

Party Music

Nadine opened the front door and stared at the police officer waiting for her.

"Are you here to stop the party or join it?" she asked.

"The music is too loud, Miss," he said.

"No. The music is hypnotic," she replied.

Only one of them was right. Hint: it's the one riding a naked man.

Who's Counting?

Jack closed his eyes.

Alicia opened her eyes.

Alicia closed her eyes.

Trent opened his eyes.

Trent closed his eyes.

Marge opened her eyes.

Marge closed her eyes.

"Oh, wow! I had no idea you had installed so many different personalities on your brother," Katherine said. "What's your record?"

"Sixty-nine, but who's counting?" Allison chuckled.

Bullseye!

Jonathan stared in awe at the dartboard.

"I lost?" he gasped. "Impossible! I never lose!"

"You do now," Gladys retorted.

"You messed with my head! That's the only explanation!"

"No, I messed with your cock," she snapped her fingers.

Erection raging out of control, Jonathan dropped the darts on the floor as she said,

"Bullseye!"

Not Her Fault

"Please don't make me do this," Henry begged.

"I'm not making you do anything," Cindy replied.

"Yes, you are. You're inside my mind!"

"You're the one that put me there. Those recordings weren't for you."

"Fuck!" Henry sobbed as he left the house, wearing nothing but a dog mask. The neighborhood is still in shock.

Nocturnal Visit

"What am I looking at?" Brian asked, staring at footage from Jake's camera.

"Wait for it... There!"

"Fuck! Was that a flying woman?"

"It's a demon."

"How do you know?"

"She paid me a visit after I saw her and now it's your turn. Feed her well..." Jake grinned.

A clawed hand touched Brian's neck.

Mistress Angel is Amazing

The latest post draft read,

Mistress Angel is amazing.

I worship Mistress Angel.

I'll do anything for Mistress Angel.

Harrison read it one last time and then posted it once, twice, three times, until his website was a giant devotional mural. He loved her so fucking much!

Too bad he didn't remember ever meeting her.

Empty Box

Getting a present from Goddess was always a treat but the box was...

"Empty?" Madison grumbled. "Why? Have I done anything to displease you?"

"No, dear," Goddess Tania smiled. "This box and your mind have a lot in common, don't they?"

"Yes," the slave girl replied, dropping into the blissful trance again. Everything was perfect.

Perfect Math

"Preposterous!" Rudy squinted.

"What?" Marge asked.

"The math on this paper doesn't make any sense."

"On the contrary, dear."

"So, eleven minus two is three?"

"Of course."

"And six times six is two?"

"Definitely."

"And eight plus seven is one?"

"Yes, and you've just reached zero."´

Rudy immediately dropped into a trance. Everything checked out.

To Dye For

"Did you change your hair color again?" Thomas asked.

"Yes," Dorothy replied. "Do you like it?"

"No, pink doesn't suit you."

"Do you prefer blue?"

"No, I..." he blinked. "Hey, how did you do that?"

"Do what?"

"Your hair is..."

"Green?"

Thomas shook his head, even more confused. Her hypnotic suggestions were to dye for.

Premature Theft

Harold stared blankly at the empty office safe.

"I was never here," the cat burglar waved her latex gloves, deepening the trance.

"Yes, Mistress," he replied.

"Good boy. Stroke your cock as I take my leave. You'll only wake up when you cum."

Five seconds later...

"Fuck!" she grumbled as he sounded the alarm.

New Programming

"God, please no!" James begged.

The laptop was frozen, stuck in the middle of an update. Countless horror stories of bricked machines invaded his thoughts.

"Please work..."

An hour later, the screen became a mesh of moving spirals dominated by his sister's cerulean eyes.

The new programming is still underway. His mind will never recover.

On the Surface

Cameron was amazed.

"Did you ever expect to see humans on Mars?" Theresa asked.

"No, but I'm confused," he replied.

"About what?"

"Why are their suits sticking to the ground like that?"

"The surface is made of chewing gum."

"Makes sense."

"Only for your entranced mind," she thought.

He continued staring at a blank screen.

Not a Table

Whatever Nathan had built, it wasn't a table.

"Why didn't you follow the instructions?" Clark asked.

"Because they're written in gibberish!"

"Where's the paper?" Valerie intervened.

"Huh?" Nathan scratched his chin.

"And the wood?" she insisted.

Both men stared at the empty kitchen, united in the same thought.

"Where are our minds?" they mumbled.

"Exactly."

The Perfect Number

This sentence is six words long.

This one is only five.

However, this one goes all the way up to ten.

You follow the numbers, wondering where they lead.

Sometimes, up.

Sometimes, down.

Numbers are infinite, but only one is perfect.

See it now as the fantasy takes over.

Zero.

No thoughts.

No mind.

Sleep!

This Was Your Idea

Alan stared at Denise's cum-filled boobs as she fucked his cousin Paul in the ass atop their kitchen table.

"This is not what I had in mind for entertainment tonight..." he said.

"On the contrary, dear, this was your idea," girlfriend Anya replied.

"I don't remember that."

"I know. Isn't hypnosis hot?"

He mindlessly agreed.

No Reflection

Jake's reflection in the mirror was gone which could only mean...

"I'm a vampire? Fuck! You did this!" he turned to Marge in anger. "Undo it immediately."

"It doesn't work like that, boy," she waved her dark fingernails.

"Then I'm really stuck like this forever?"

"No. Only until the hypnotic suggestion wears off," she thought.

Finally Over

It was finally over. Walter looked at the mangled witch's body one last time before setting it on fire, burning the last remnants of her iniquity with it.

Or so he thought.

Sweat dripping from his furrowed brow, he drove away. He didn't see the black shadow glued to his head, feasting on every thought.

Bureaucratic Nightmare

The paperwork kept piling up, a cascade of boredom threatening to swallow Richard whole.

"Please, stop!" he begged.

"Are you ready to obey?" Daphne asked.

"Yes! Anything you want!"

"I'll hold you to that," she snapped her fingers.

Richard woke up from a trance and smiled. He had never been happier to see a broom.

Clean Slate

Mark looked inside his mind. The clutter was gone.

"You did it!" he turned to Angela.

"Of course. I'm an expert."

"Clean slate, huh?"

"Yes, dear."

"One question, though. When you removed those thoughts from my head, did you plant some of yours too?"

"Why do you ask?"

"I'm kneeling and can't get up."

"Perfect."

Completely Mesmerized

Richard stared at the TV, seeing nothing but static.

"Is it over?" he asked.

"The contest ended a couple of hours ago, yes," Samantha replied.

"Why don't I remember a single song?"

"They were so good you were completely mesmerized, dear."

"Right..."

They both started laughing. She was a wonderful hypnotist, but a terrible liar.

Poor Bastard

The X-ray results were surprising.

"Oh wow," Dr. Cartwright said. "I've never seen anything stuck so deep. How did it happen?"

"The patient claims he was hypnotized by his wife. She demanded and... "

"... he obeyed. Did she tell him to swallow all that junk too?"

"No, she didn't..."

"Good."

"... but she had friends staying over."

Fallacy

The winning hand was Emily's... again!

"Fuck this!" Brandon shouted, throwing his glass against the wall. "How?"

"I guess I'm lucky," she replied.

"Lucky, my ass! You hypnotized me again, didn't you?"

"No. Again is a fallacy if you never stopped being in trance. "Shirt next, please."

Brandon sighed, hoping for the game to end.

No One Will Believe…

The extras for Maureen's new movie were all lined up for Thomas to see and their costumes sucked.

"What do you mean?" she asked.

"They just do. No one will believe they're vampires looking at them."

"Exactly what I wanted to hear. Thank you, my dear."

"Huh? Why?"

Fangs glistened in the shadows around him...

Disobedience

Gregory waited anxiously inside the empty elevator.

"Do we really need to do this?" he asked.

"Yes," his hypnotic Mistress replied. "Disobedience is always punished."

"But..."

"No more whining," she snapped her fingers. "Obey."

"Yes, Mistress."

The doors opened to his company's costume party. The naked man was the center of attention all night long.

Delicacies of the Mind

The rose ice cream was fresh and tasty. Alan was impressed.

"You actually did this?" he asked.

"Yes. I learned a lot of things during the lockdown," Harriet replied.

"What else did you learn?"

"How to hypnotize people."

"Cool."

"Damn right it is," she smiled as he continued putting the imaginary spoon into his mouth.

Inevitable

It was happening everywhere. Men were women's mindless drones and all because of the...

"... new vaccine," Quentin concluded, looking at the swelling on his left shoulder. "Shit!"

"It's too late to stop it now," his girlfriend said, decked in a nurse's outfit. "You're mine. Enjoy the ride."

Quentin screamed as his individuality ceased to exist.

Welcoming Eternity

She sat, eyes closed, listening to Beauty. The time-traveling hypnotist thought she knew it all, but she was wrong.

"Have you come to hypnotize me?" the maestro asked, momentarily stepping away from his keyboards.

"This time, I'm leaving all the trances to you. Please continue."

"Gladly," he resumed his improvisations, welcoming eternity with each note.

Hypnosis Sucks!

"You seriously wasted your money learning erotic hypnosis? Why?" David asked.

"Because it's fun," Jessica replied.

"Bah! Hypnosis sucks!"

"Don't say that."

"Why not if it's true? It sucks!

"Keep that up and you'll be sorry..."

"Oh yeah? Hypnosis fucking sucks!"

David sucked her collection of dildos all weekend long. She's purchasing more right now.

Enjoy Your Weekend

Amanda's new music video was horrible. Poor production values, improper sound mixing, forgettable wardrobe... yet Gerald kept watching it over and over. Why?

"Subliminal messages," she smiled, "You're hooked!"

"Absurd!" he retorted. "And I can stop whenever I want."

"Said every addict in the world... Enjoy your weekend."

He did. Five hundred views and counting.

Secret Ingredient

"These cupcakes are delicious, Jenna!" Matthew declared.

"Thank you. I'm glad you like the special ingredient."

"What is it?"

"If I tell you, it's not a secret anymore."

"Oh, come on!"

"Okay, it's your cum!"

"What?"

"Yes. What better way to program you to eat your load for me?"

Matthew gasped... and took another bite.

Feeling Peckish

Bob stared at the shadow in front of him.

"You're not my wife," he said.

"I never said I was," she smirked.

"What do you want?"

"Your mind, for starters. I'm feeling peckish."

"No. I'm no one's meal."

"I was thinking more of an appetizer."

His thoughts started deliquescing before he had time to scream.

Amazing Pictures

Lucy's pictures were to die for. Whenever Jake thought they couldn't get any better, she surprised him with another hot set.

"Hmm, so good..." he moaned.

"What do you like the most about these?" she asked.

"Latex catsuits are amazing."

"Latex, huh?" she chuckled. "Cool."

Jake continued to stare lovingly at her 'Fat Bastard' suit.

Ringtone

Mistress Cornelia's hypnotic ringtone was first downloaded by Sheila Adams who had her friend Barbara listen to it the minute after.

An hour later, more than five thousand people had already heard the entrancing sound.

As I type this, the drone army keeps growing. I shattered my phone, but my ears still work. Mercy, please!

Scratch Marks

It had taken forever, but her pet had quieted down.

"Finally!" Martha exclaimed.

"Trouble in hypnotic paradise?" Jane asked.

"Something like that."

"What happened?"

"I finally convinced Nathan he was my cat..."

"Congratulations!"

"... but he also believed he was in heat."

"Ouch!"

"Yeah..." Martha dragged herself across the room, scratch marks all over her body.

Book Reading

It was the book reading everyone was waiting for, but it was over the moment it began. When confronted about what had happened, author Beth Warner replied,

"All I did was read the first line of the novel."

"Which is...?"

"You are all completely asleep and under my control."

The journalists collapsed at her feet.

Conclusion

How was the meal? Scrumptious, right? Good. However, this is only the beginning.

If you want to have even more fun with these little fantasies of the mind, then head to my personal website - https://www.sbspellbound.net – and explore everything else I have to offer there. New content every day, new ideas always blooming. Support my creative efforts if you wish to see more. See you there.

www.ingramcontent.com/pod-product-compliance
Lightning Source LLC
Chambersburg PA
CBHW060912130726

48001CB00006B/2204